Samuel French Acting Edition

I0591783

The Party

by Sally Potter

SAMUELFRENCH.COM   SAMUELFRENCH.CO.UK

FOR PRODUCTION ENQUIRIES

UNITED STATES AND CANADA
Info@SamuelFrench.com
1-866-598-8449

UNITED KINGDOM AND EUROPE
Plays@SamuelFrench.co.uk
020-7255-4302

Each title is subject to availability from Samuel French, depending upon country of performance. Please be aware that *THE PARTY* may not be licensed by Samuel French in your territory. Professional and amateur producers should contact the nearest Samuel French office or licensing partner to verify availability.

MUSIC USE NOTE

Licensees are solely responsible for obtaining formal written permission from copyright owners to use copyrighted music in the performance of this play and are strongly cautioned to do so. If no such permission is obtained by the licensee, then the licensee must use only original music that the licensee owns and controls. Licensees are solely responsible and liable for all music clearances and shall indemnify the copyright owners of the play(s) and their licensing agent, Samuel French, against any costs, expenses, losses and liabilities arising from the use of music by licensees. Please contact the appropriate music licensing authority in your territory for the rights to any incidental music.

IMPORTANT BILLING AND CREDIT REQUIREMENTS

If you have obtained performance rights to this title, please refer to your licensing agreement for important billing and credit requirements.

CHARACTERS

JANET – a politician, just promoted to Shadow Minister for Health in the Opposition Party

BILL – Janet's husband, an academic

APRIL – Janet's closest friend, an elegant professional and ex-activist

GOTTFRIED – April's German partner, a healer and life coach

MARTHA – Bill's oldest friend, a professor

JINNY – Martha's younger wife, a chef

TOM – a banker, husband of Janet's colleague Marianne

SETTING

All the action takes place in one house in London. The house is comfortable but not wealthy; it looks lived in but not particularly well-maintained. These are evidently culturally and politically active people, well-read and with eclectic musical taste.

The front door of the house opens into a hallway with doors that lead into three rooms: a kitchen, a bathroom, and a living room (lots of books, a vinyl record collection, and a chair carefully placed between two stereo speakers), with French doors leading from the living room into a small backyard.

The only design stipulation for any production is that the audience must be able to witness activity happening simultaneously in each of the different rooms. The precise geography of the house (and its backyard) are open to ingenuity and interpretation.

This will, of course, partly depend on the performance venue and scale of the production. A rotating stage, for example, would allow us to look into the relevant combinations of rooms at any given moment; a two-storied house (like looking into a doll's house) would allow us to see into all of the rooms all the time; whilst a more minimal approach would be to define different areas of the stage purely with light and sound and a minimal use of props and furniture.

TIME

The present. The action unfolds in continuous time.

AUTHOR'S NOTE

Music and Choreography

The music tracks indicated are those originally chosen for the film, though other similar pieces should be used if licensees are unable to acquire the rights to any of the songs under copyright. The music is, in effect, the soundtrack to Bill's life; a catalogue of his longings, often used in counterpoint to the unfolding events.

Moments of synchronicity in the way people move, sit, or are suddenly still can indicate connections between individuals that they are not aware of – like hidden threads joining them. This can be pushed toward a choreography of everyday gesture, along with the movement of individuals from one room to another.

Changes of sound level, reflecting the characters' subjective experiences and the acoustic reality of each room, will clarify how the spaces interconnect and enhance the accelerating pace of the action.

MUSIC LIST

As stated in the Author's Note, the following songs are those originally chosen for the film. A license to produce *The Party* does not include a performance license for any third-party or copyrighted music. The publisher and author suggest that the licensee contact ASCAP or BMI to ascertain the music publishers and contact such music publishers to license or acquire permission for performance of the following songs. If a license or permission is unattainable for these songs, the licensee may not use them in *The Party*, but should create original compositions in a similar style or use similar songs in the public domain.

Music Cue 1: "Jerusalem," adapted for electric guitar

Music Cue 2: "I'm a Man" by Bo Diddley

Music Cue 3: "What is This Thing Called Love" by Sidney Bechet

Music Cue 4: "Como Siento Yo" by Rubén González

Music Cue 5: "Summertime" played by Albert Ayler

Music Cue 6: "Ay Candela" by Ibrahim Ferrer and Los Bocucos

Music Cue 7: "My One and Only Love" played by John Coltrane

Music Cue 8: "Surfin'" by Ernest Ranglin

Music Cue 9: "When I am Laid in Earth" Dido's Lament by Henry Purcell

Music Cue 10: "Ciocirlia" by Grigoraş Dinicu et son orchestra

Music Cue 11: "Canção Verdes Anos" by Carlos Paredes

Music Cue 12: "Emancipacion" by Osvaldo Pugliese

[MUSIC CUE 1]

(It is night. The front door of the house opens to reveal **JANET** *– wild-eyed, standing trembling in the open doorway. She slowly lifts a gun and points it at the anonymous, unseen arrival.)*

(Blackout.)

(When the lights come up we can see into a hallway and three rooms that open into it: a kitchen, a living room, and a small bathroom. The last rays of early evening sunlight flood into the rooms through windows that overlook a backyard.)

*(***BILL** *is sitting slumped in a chair in the living room. He twirls a glass of wine back and forth then gulps down the contents and refills it from a bottle by the chair. He looks troubled.)*

*(***JANET**, *wearing an apron over a skirt and blouse, is busying herself in the adjacent kitchen preparing some pastry cases. Her phone rings. She pulls it out from its customary position tucked inside her blouse.)*

JANET. Hello. Yes! It's true!

(She laughs excitedly.)

*(***BILL** *sits, listening to* **JANET**'s *bright, automatic voice through the open door. It's hard to tell if he is admiring or critical of her remarks.)*

Well, I had an inkling, but it was still sort of a surprise... and what an honor. Yes. I hope I can live up to it. Such a responsibility. Huge, actually.

BILL. *(Murmuring.)* Huge.

> *(JANET tucks her phone away, but it rings again immediately.)*
>
> *(BILL rises slowly to his feet, crosses the room, and lowers a needle carefully onto a long-playing record on a turntable.*

[MUSIC CUE 2]

> *(It's classic rhythm and blues; heavy, rhythmic, and loud.)*
>
> *(BILL staggers back across the room and sits down heavily in his chair opposite his stereo speakers.)*

JANET. Hello. Oh thank you so much.

> *(She listens to the voice at the other end, grimaces, and then answers brightly:)*

No, not at all – it's fine. A good moment. Please – don't apologize. It's good of you to call. Oh – I haven't decided yet, but you're top of my list. Oh, absolutely. You've been marvelous.

> *(BILL listens to JANET's cheery, diplomatic tone with a weary expression.)*

BILL. *(Sarcastically.)* Marvelous.

JANET. Thanks again. Have to dash but – don't worry, I won't forget you!

> *(She's about to put her phone away when it rings again. She looks at the screen before being distracted by a loud knock at the door.)*
>
> *(She walks out of the kitchen into the hallway and looks through the open doorway into the living room.)*

Bill! Bill!

> *(She points at her phone, gesturing for BILL to turn down the volume of the music. With a weary smile he drags himself to his feet,*

crosses the room, and takes the record off the turntable. There's a brief moment of silence as **JANET** *opens the front door, still clutching her phone.)*

(It's **APRIL** *and* **GOTTFRIED**. **APRIL** *is immaculately made-up and well-dressed.* **GOTTFRIED** *hovers behind her holding a bunch of flowers and a couple of bottles of champagne. He is smiling broadly. Professionally.)*

(**APRIL** *spreads her arms wide and smiles at* **JANET**.*)*

April!

APRIL. Janet!

Congratulations, darling. You did it.

(**BILL**, *standing hunched over the turntable, glances in their direction then lowers the needle onto another record.)*

[MUSIC CUE 3]

(**APRIL** *and* **JANET** *hug warmly.)*

GOTTFRIED. My condolences, Janet.

(He hands **JANET** *the flowers with a little bow.)*

Because once you've reached the top of the mountain, you can only go –

(He gestures downwards as **BILL** *simultaneously sits down heavily in his chair in the living room.)*

APRIL. – Oh shut up, Gottfried. Spare us the aphorisms. You're a star, Janet, and I'm proud of you, even though I think democracy is finished.

JANET. Thanks, April. At least you're consistent.

(They walk down the hallway past the living room door. **BILL** *raises his glass at them and points questioningly at the half-empty bottle of wine.)*

GOTTFRIED. Actually, I'm not drinking alcohol at the moment.

APRIL. Tosser.

> (**APRIL** *grabs the bottles of champagne from* **GOTTFRIED** *and follows* **JANET** *into the kitchen.*)

> (**GOTTFRIED** *hesitates then heads into the living room. He looks around then lowers himself onto the carpet and sits cross-legged opposite* **BILL**.)

> (*In the kitchen,* **APRIL** *puts the bottles of champagne in the fridge. She looks* **JANET** *up and down appraisingly as* **JANET** *arranges Gottfried's bunch of flowers in a vase.*)

So. Do you feel different yet?

JANET. No, not really.

APRIL. I suppose you do look *slightly* ministerial in that pinny, in a twenty-first-century post-modern, post-post-feminist sort of way.

JANET. It hasn't really sunk in yet. I've been so busy...

> (*Her phone rings again. She pulls it out from her blouse, glancing at the screen before answering.*)

Hi Mum. You did, yes, you always did. Yes, he's very proud. He has. He's been really supportive. Terrific. Yes. I know. I *am* lucky.

> (**APRIL** *smiles ironically.*)

Listen, Mum, I've got guests over. Can I call you a bit later?

> (*In the living room,* **BILL** *stirs and looks at* **GOTTFRIED** *blearily. He gestures vaguely at the bottle of wine.*)

BILL. Sure you don't want...?

> (**GOTTFRIED** *shakes his head, smiling. There's an awkward pause.*)

(Murmuring.) You are...?

GOTTFRIED. Gottfried.

> (**BILL** *nods.*)

BILL. Ah, yes. Yes... And I'm Bill, I think. Well, I used to be.

> (**GOTTFRIED** *laughs.*)

GOTTFRIED. That's very funny.

BILL. It wasn't a joke.

> (**GOTTFRIED** *smiles warmly at* **BILL.** *That professional smile.*)

GOTTFRIED. Oh. Okay. I hear you.

> (**GOTTFRIED** *breathes deeply then closes his eyes.* **BILL** *looks at him for a while with a bleary, puzzled expression. The two men sit motionless, each in their own world as the music plays.*)

> (**APRIL** *drifts elegantly from the kitchen into the living room and sees* **GOTTFRIED** *sitting cross-legged, his eyes closed.*)

APRIL. Please tell me you're not meditating, Gottfried. Pull yourself together.

> (**GOTTFRIED** *opens his eyes and smiles lovingly at* **APRIL.**)

Sorry about my German boyfriend, Bill. But we're in the middle of separating, just so you know.

> *(There's a knock at the door.)*

JANET. *(Shouting.)* April, can you?

> (**APRIL** *heads toward the front door.* **GOTTFRIED** *smiles at* **BILL.**)

GOTTFRIED. She is so beautiful.

BILL. Who?

GOTTFRIED. April. I am a very lucky man.

> (**APRIL** *opens the front door. It's* **MARTHA**; *professional, vigorous, sharp haircut. She grins at* **APRIL.**)

APRIL. Martha! All by yourself? Where's your wife?

MARTHA. On her way. She's scanning, actually. Where's Janet?

APRIL. Doing a Thatcher. Proving she can still rustle up a canapé in the kitchen when necessary, despite her political prowess.

> (**APRIL** *gestures toward the kitchen then heads into the living room, glancing at* **GOTTFRIED** *with a disapproving expression before taking up a position by the mantelpiece.*)

> (**MARTHA** *walks into the kitchen where* **JANET** *is bending down, sliding a tray of pastry cases into the oven.*)

MARTHA. Oh, Janet, it is wonderful and marvelous. A triumph for womankind.

> (*She kisses* **JANET** *on the cheek.*)

Well, for any kind, come to that. At last your ailing party has a person at the helm of health who has principles as well as ambition.

JANET. Well, thank you, Martha. You look as if you really mean that.

MARTHA. Of course I do, you fool. I am very proud of you. As I know Bill is.

> (**MARTHA** *grins at* **JANET** *then marches into the living room. She punches* **BILL** *on the arm affectionately.*)

Letting Janet do the catering are you? That's good of you. I suppose you're exhausted from all these years of being so perfect.

APRIL. (*Murmuring.*) Arguable.

MARTHA. Well, it was worth it, you brilliant bastard. She's made it to the top. Congratulations, you old failure, you.

> (*Janet's phone rings again.*)

GOTTFRIED. Behind every successful woman, there is a –

APRIL. – Oh, shut up, Gottfried. Your clichés are unbearable.

> *(In the kitchen, **JANET** speaks to the latest caller brightly whilst arranging some champagne glasses on a tray.)*

JANET. Hello! Thank you so much. Oh – that's very kind of you, but I can't do tonight...what a shame. We're celebrating at home with a few close friends, actually. Which you absolutely are too, of course. But – look – how about tomorrow?

> *(In the living room, **MARTHA** looks at **APRIL** and shakes her head.)*

MARTHA. Everyone's going to want a piece of Jan, now. They'll eat her alive.

APRIL. Don't worry about her. Looks like a girl, thinks like a man, androgynous soul, always had true grit. Sounds like me, come to think of it. But the difference between us is this: Janet actually believes change is achievable through parliamentary politics.

> *(**APRIL** looks down at **BILL** sitting immobile in his chair.)*

You're rather quiet this evening, Bill.

> *(**BILL** stares glassily ahead, lost in his own world. Janet's phone rings again.)*

> *(In the kitchen, **JANET** looks at her screen, crosses to the window, and giggles flirtatiously.)*

JANET. *(Whispering.)* Will you please stop calling! Stop it! It's impossible to talk, people keep coming in and out.

> *(She glances anxiously toward the living room then steps toward the kitchen door and speaks exaggeratedly loud for the benefit of the others.)*

Terrific! Well, I'll see you tomorrow morning then! Looking forward to it!

> *(She returns to her place by the window.)*

JANET. *(Whispering.)* Bye. I'm going. Right now. Stop it! I'm ringing off. Now! Bye bye.

> *(A flurry of knocks at the front door.* APRIL *and* MARTHA *both move toward the living room door, but* APRIL *puts out a hand to block* MARTHA.*)*

APRIL. My job. I am the gatekeeper, by order of the minister.

> *(*APRIL *marches down the hall to the front door and flings it open.* JINNY *is standing outside the front door. She looks flushed, excited.)*

Jinny.

JINNY. Oh hi, April, hi!

> *(*APRIL *looks her up and down as she steps into the hallway.)*

APRIL. You still look pretty slim. Considering.

JINNY. *(Breathlessly.)* Listen. Has Martha arrived yet?

> *(*APRIL *closes the front door and gestures airily toward the living room.)*

APRIL. She's in there, thumping her old pal. Janet's in the kitchen if you want to –

JINNY. – No thanks. I really want to see Martha. Now.

APRIL. You're missing her *that* much? Marriage really is an insufferably smug institution.

JINNY. *(Defensively.)* I like it.

APRIL. Well, Gottfried and I are separating.

> *(*APRIL *pokes her head around the living room door.)*

(Pointedly.) This is our last supper.

> *(*MARTHA *gets up and opens her arms wide as* JINNY *enters the room. But* JINNY *freezes melodramatically.)*

MARTHA. What's up, Jin?

> *(*JINNY *lifts three fingers.)*

Excuse me?

JINNY. *(In a stage whisper.)* Three, Martha, three.

> *(Her eyes are wide with excitement, or fright.)*

MARTHA. Excuse us…

> *(**MARTHA** puts her arm around **JINNY**'s shoulders and guides her through the French doors into the backyard.)*

> *(**BILL** gets up and staggers over to the turntable, where he changes the record.)*

[MUSIC CUE 4]

> *(**APRIL** is standing in the kitchen doorway watching **JANET**, who is peering out of the kitchen window at **JINNY** and **MARTHA** in a huddle in the backyard.)*

APRIL. So who else is coming?

> *(**JANET** glances back over her shoulder at **APRIL**.)*

JANET. Just Tom and Marianne.

> *(**APRIL** sits down at the kitchen table as **JANET** busies herself at the kitchen stove, her back to **APRIL**.)*

APRIL. The beautiful Marianne, the queen of spin. And that ridiculously handsome husband of hers. Too bad he's a wanker banker with the mysterious ability to make millions out of others' misfortunes. Why on earth have you invited them?

JANET. She and I will work together from now on. You know, cooperate?

> *(**JANET** turns briefly and smiles over her shoulder at **APRIL**.)*

APRIL. You mean you'll be her boss?

JANET. Well I don't actually use that word, but yes, I suppose so.

APRIL. So she will be your underling, taking copious notes whilst plotting how to take your place one day.

JANET. She and I are on very good terms, actually. We'll be sharing an office from now on.

APRIL. Lucky you. Gazing on all that genetic good fortune.

(**JANET** *turns around and looks directly at* **APRIL.**)

JANET. April…

(**APRIL** *studies* **JANET**'s *serious expression.*)

APRIL. Janet.

JANET. *(Quietly.)* Do you think Bill's all right? I mean this is what we've always wanted – well, I always wanted and he's always encouraged me – but now he seems –

APRIL. – Drunk?

JANET. Depressed.

APRIL. Oh, don't worry about him. Look. If Dennis Thatcher and Prince Philip could trail along behind their female leaders without complaint then so can Bill.

(*The phone rings again.* **JANET** *picks it up automatically just as there's a knock at the front door.*)

JANET. Hello. Thank you. Thank you so much for calling.

(**APRIL** *sets off briskly down the hallway and opens the front door with a flourish, smiling.* **TOM** *is standing outside. He is handsome, well-groomed, and wearing a very good suit, but seems agitated.*)

TOM. *(Smiling exaggeratedly.)* Oh, April. How lovely to see you. It's been…it's been too long.

(**APRIL** *nods her head politely.*)

APRIL. Possibly. Are you alone? Where's Marianne?

TOM. Marianne's been delayed, unfortunately. She sends her apologies. She's going to try to get here in time for dessert.

APRIL. Oh. Marvelous.

> (**APRIL** *doesn't move. She's surveying his suit, studying his face.*)

TOM. Or cheese.

APRIL. Terrific.

> (*But she's still not letting him pass.*)

TOM. Or coffee, perhaps.

APRIL. Smashing.

> (**APRIL** *stands aside at last.* **TOM** *steps inside the house as* **APRIL** *sets off down the hallway.*)

TOM. April, where's the bathroom, please?

> (**APRIL** *stops in her tracks, turns around, and points at the closed bathroom door.*)

APRIL. Lavatory.

> (*She points at the open kitchen doorway.*)

Kitchen. Hostess.

> (*She points at the open door leading into the living room.*)

Host.

> (**APRIL** *walks into the kitchen and shuts the door behind her.*)

> (**TOM** *steps forward and peers tentatively into the living room.* **BILL** *is bending over his turntable again.*)

[MUSIC CUE 5]

> (*Jazz. A wild, wailing saxophone.*)

> (**TOM** *recoils, hesitates, then darts into the bathroom. He locks the door behind him and leans back against it, breathing heavily.*)

> (*In the kitchen,* **APRIL** *sits down at the table.*)

That was Tom. He's in the lavatory. Wearing an extremely expensive suit.

> (**JANET** *crosses the kitchen and stands by the sink, her back to* **APRIL**.)

JANET. No Marianne?

APRIL. Later. Pity. Meanwhile, Bill seems to be running some sort of disco. Oh, I hope Gottfried isn't dancing. I'd better check.

> (*She gets up, leaves the kitchen, and walks into the living room, where* **GOTTFRIED** *is now lying on the floor.* **APRIL** *steps over him fastidiously and sits down on the sofa.*)

> (*In the bathroom,* **TOM** *turns on the light. He takes some lavatory paper and rapidly wipes the side of the bath then kneels down by the bath and reaches into his jacket pocket.*)

> (*He empties a small packet of white powder onto the side of the bath.*)

> (*His hands are shaking as he whips out a credit card, chopping the powder briskly, dividing it into lines.*)

> (*In the kitchen,* **JANET** *is chopping some mushrooms equally briskly. Her phone rings. She stops chopping and lifts the phone to her ear.*)

JANET. *(Whispering.)* Please. Stop! No more. Me too, me too. Soon.

> (**JANET** *makes a kissing sound into the phone then tucks it back into her blouse, smiling to herself.*)

> (*In the bathroom,* **TOM** *bends down and inhales the lines of powder deeply then arches back.*)

TOM. Ah. Ah.

> (*He gets up and paces about, jittery and high, then takes off his jacket and hangs it carefully on a hook on the back of the door.*

A gun is strapped to his body in a stiff, shiny, new-looking holster. He takes it out, stares at it, then practices pulling it in and out of the holster a few times. He drops the cartridge onto the floor. He's clearly not used to handling a gun.)

(Muttering.) You're not a loser, Tom. Not a loser.

*(**TOM** stares at his reflection in the cabinet mirror and opens and closes his mouth, massaging his gums. He inspects a towel, sniffing it cautiously, before wrapping it carefully around his middle to protect his immaculate trousers. Then he splashes his face again and again with cold water before drying his face gingerly with the towel.)*

(He opens the cupboard door above the sink, inspects the contents, takes out a bottle of deodorant, opens his shirt, and sprays wildly under his arms, wincing at the smell.)

(Murmuring.) Cheap. Fucking cheap.

*(He slams the cupboard door shut then, after one last glance in the mirror, leaves the bathroom. He crosses the hallway and peers in through the living room door. The wailing saxophone blares out from the speakers at the other end of the room as **GOTTFRIED** and **APRIL** sit stiffly at either end of the sofa and **BILL** sits slumped in his chair.)*

*(**TOM** turns around, pushes open the kitchen door, and slams it behind him, startling **JANET**.)*

Janet! Wonderful, wonderful news.

*(**JANET** wheels around to face **TOM**, holding the chopping knife in front of her, pointing it defensively at him.)*

(**TOM** *raises his arms in mock surrender. Smiling, over-friendly:*)

TOM. I'm not a bit surprised.

JANET. Really?

(**JANET** *looks down modestly and continues her chopping. She shrugs.*)

Well, I am.

TOM. Surely not.

JANET. Let's see what I can achieve once I get going.

TOM. You're too modest. Oh...by the way, Marianne has been delayed. Just a –

JANET. – She works so hard.

TOM. She sends her apologies. But she'll try and get here later on.

JANET. Oh, good. How nice.

TOM. For coffee.

JANET. Lovely.

TOM. If she can.

(**JANET** *looks up and smiles brightly at* **TOM.**)

JANET. Terrific. A drink Tom? I'll get you a drink!

TOM. No no no. You're busy. Stay where you are. I'll join the others. Shall I? Unless you want some help?

JANET. Oh, no no no.

TOM. Okay. Right. Well, then – where's that marvelous husband of yours, Janet?

(**JANET** *points with her little knife in the direction of the living room.*)

Right. Got it. Congratulations again, Janet.

(**TOM** *unwraps some chewing gum and throws it into his mouth then leaves the room, slamming the door behind him.*)

(*In the backyard,* **MARTHA** *and* **JINNY** *are standing near some dustbins. The atmosphere between them is strained.*)

JINNY. Martha! Look at me!

> (*But* **MARTHA** *is avoiding* **JINNY**'s *imploring gaze.*)

It's wonderful, isn't it?

MARTHA. (*Hesitantly.*) Jinny...

JINNY. It's what we always wanted, isn't it?

MARTHA. Oh, Jinny...

JINNY. Will you tell them? I'm so excited, I feel I could burst!

> (**JINNY**'s *face changes to an expression of horror.*)

Oh, god, will I burst?

> (*The two women meet each other's gaze then fling their arms around each other. Neither can see the other's expression:* **JINNY** *looks excitedly anxious, whilst* **MARTHA** *looks seriously worried.*)

MARTHA. I guess we're about to become a collective. Just when I'd got used to the idea of us being a couple.

> (**JINNY** *pulls away from* **MARTHA**'s *embrace. She looks pained.*)

JINNY. Martha. We're going to be a *family*. Will you tell them please? Will you tell them how happy we are?

> (*In the living room,* **BILL** *is leaning over the music system, changing the record and pushing the volume up again.*)

[MUSIC CUE 6]

> (**BILL** *glances at* **TOM**, *who is now sitting bolt-upright on a chair at the back of the room, staring at* **BILL** *with an expression of loathing whilst mechanically chewing some gum, his leg jiggling impatiently.*)

> (*In the kitchen,* **JANET** *takes the champagne out of the fridge, puts it on the tray with the*

*glasses, and carries it into the living room.
She hands the tray to* **APRIL**, *crosses the room,
and switches the light on next to* **BILL**. *He
jumps.)*

JANET. *(Pointedly.)* Could you maybe come and help me for
just a *minute*, darling?

(**BILL** *turns to look at her, swaying slightly.)*

Are you all right?

(**MARTHA** *and* **JINNY** *suddenly re-appear
through the French doors, their arms wrapped
around each other.)*

MARTHA. *(In a loud voice.)* We have an announcement.

(**GOTTFRIED**, **APRIL**, **BILL**, *and* **JANET** *all turn
to look at* **MARTHA**. *She gestures toward the
sound system.)*

Bill, I know you adore that thing, but could you?

(**BILL** *reluctantly turns down the volume of the
music. Everyone looks at* **MARTHA**, *waiting for
her to speak. She hesitates, glances at* **JINNY**,
and then begins.)

So. Everybody. It seems that we are expecting not one,
not two, but three babies. People. Small people.

(There's an awkward pause. **JANET** *is the first
to break the silence, smiling brightly:)*

JANET. Oh. Well, congratulations. Wow.

(**JANET** *walks over and hugs* **MARTHA** *and*
JINNY *warmly.* **BILL** *staggers back to his chair.)*

BILL. *(Dully.)* Wow.

TOM. *(Muttering.)* Awesome.

(**APRIL** *picks up one of the bottles of
champagne.)*

APRIL. Was that a boast or a cry for help, Martha? Couldn't
quite tell, from your tone of voice.

GOTTFRIED. *(Dreamily.)* The miracle of conception...

APRIL. Oh, shut up, Gottfried.

> (**APRIL** *starts to unwrap the foil from the neck of the champagne bottle.*)

Listen. I am about to propose a toast to my oldest, dearest and most loyal friend, who has achieved a rare thing, which is why we are all here this evening, in case anyone forgot. Babies – excuse me Jinny, Martha – but babies get born every day, in extremely large numbers, to the point of endangering the planet and all our futures. It's not every day, however, that one of us becomes a minister...in your entirely rotten and useless Opposition Party.

MARTHA. Oh fuck you, April.

> *(She smiles broadly.)*

Though of course you're right.

JINNY. What? Martha!

> (**JINNY** *pulls away from* **MARTHA.**)

> (**APRIL** *opens the bottle of champagne decisively. The cork flies through the air like a bullet, shattering the glass in one of the French doors. The others stare at the broken window incredulously.*)

MARTHA. I've never seen that happen before.

JINNY. Neither have I. Oh dear. I hope it's not an omen.

> (**JANET** *picks up a wastepaper basket and bends down to pick up the shards of glass.* **JINNY** *hovers next to her, staring down at the fragments with a worried expression, clutching her belly.*)

They look very sharp. Like knives. Pity about the window.

> (**JANET** *smiles up at her brightly.*)

JANET. Oh don't worry Jinny, it's nothing, really. Nothing. Compared to your amazing news.

GOTTFRIED. Exactly. Oh bravo, Janet. It's just a broken window in a door. Not a window into anyone's soul...

> (**APRIL** *groans and starts pouring the champagne.*)
>
> (*The phone rings.* **JANET** *picks it up automatically, looks at the screen, then changes her mind and tucks it away again.*)
>
> (**APRIL** *starts handing out the glasses.* **JINNY** *takes a glass from* **APRIL**, *looks at it longingly, then crosses the room and thrusts it at* **TOM**, *who is standing conspicuously apart from the rest of the group.*)

JINNY. Here. Take mine. I'm not really drinking, in the circumstances, you see.

> (**APRIL** *stretches out her arm and hands* **JINNY** *another glass immediately.* **JINNY** *grins.*)

(*Shrugging.*) Perhaps just a symbolic sip. What do you think, Martha?

> (**MARTHA** *shrugs.*)

MARTHA. You're a free woman.

JINNY. Am I?

> (*They look at each other questioningly.*)

APRIL. Speaking of which, do take that wretched thing off, Janet.

> (**JANET** *unties her apron and throws it onto a chair with a flourish.*)
>
> (*They each raise their glasses, except* **GOTTFRIED** *– who mimes his participation, because he's not drinking – and* **BILL**, *who is still slumped in his chair, staring glassily ahead, clutching his glass of wine in one hand and a glass of champagne in the other.*)

To Janet. I may not believe in parliamentary politics, but I absolutely do believe in you.

MARTHA. Bill. Come on, chum.

> *(But **BILL** doesn't move.)*

JANET. What is it, darling?

> *(They all stare at him. The music continues softly, suddenly intrusively upbeat in the awkward atmosphere.)*
>
> *(**BILL** clears his throat before speaking.)*

BILL. *I* have an announcement.

APRIL. *(Murmuring.)* Another announcement. Good god.

BILL. It turns out I am not well.

MARTHA. Bill!

JANET. What do you mean? What's the matter?

BILL. I've had a diagnosis. Not too good, actually.

JANET. What kind of diagnosis?

BILL. Terminal.

> *(**JANET** freezes in shock. **MARTHA** turns around and lifts the needle off the record with an audible scratch. **BILL** winces.)*

TOM. *(Muttering.)* Bastard.

> *(**JINNY**, who is standing nearest to **TOM**, overhears him. **TOM** catches her eye and registers her shocked expression.)*

> *(Whispering.)* Poor bastard. I said poor bastard.

JINNY. *(Whispering.)* Oh. Right. Yes...

> *(But she looks puzzled.)*
>
> *(**JANET** puts her glass down on the carpet and bends down in front of **BILL**, trying to get him to meet her gaze, but he isn't looking at her.)*

JANET. Terminal? Did you say terminal, Bill?

BILL. Yes. Looks like I'm done for, medically speaking.

JANET. Why didn't you tell me? Oh god. How long have you known?

> *(Her phone rings again. She pulls it out from her blouse and throws it onto the carpet. She only has eyes for* **BILL***. But* **BILL** *is still avoiding her gaze.)*

JANET. What is it, exactly? What's wrong with you?

BILL. Lung, liver, leg, take your pick.

APRIL. *(Muttering.)* Good timing, Bill.

MARTHA. *(Crossly.)* Bloody hell, April.

APRIL. *(Coolly.)* So how long have you got?

BILL. No time. No time at all.

> *(***GOTTFRIED*** suddenly rises to his feet, walks over, and stands directly in front of* **BILL***.)*

GOTTFRIED. No one knows how long they will live, Bill. No one knows when they will die.

> *(***TOM*** turns on his heel and leaves the room abruptly.)*

And Western doctors, in my opinion, know nothing at all.

> *(***TOM*** noisily slams the bathroom door closed behind him.)*

TOM. Fuck! Fuck! Fuck!

> *(***TOM*** sits down heavily on the edge of the bath and puts his head in his hands.)*

> *(In the living room,* **JANET** *paces about in front of* **BILL***.)*

JANET. I'm going to resign. Immediately. Now. Well, tomorrow morning. Or as soon as they can find someone to replace me. I'm going to look after you.

BILL. *(Quietly.)* No, Janet, no.

JANET. Yes, Bill. Yes. Of course I will. You've supported me every step of the way. You gave up everything –

APRIL. – Nearly everything –

JANET. – And now I'll do the same for you.

(**JANET** *falls onto her knees in front of* **BILL**, *landing on her champagne glass with a cry of pain. She reaches down and pulls a shard of glass out of a gaping, bloody wound in her knee.*)

More! I'll do more!

APRIL. Oh Janet. Fuck.

(**JINNY** *looks aghast at Janet's bleeding knee and suddenly gags, rushing out of the living room in the direction of the bathroom, bumping into* **TOM** *as he comes back out.*)

(**TOM** *leans against the wall in the hallway, listening to the sound of* **JINNY** *retching in the bathroom.*)

TOM. Fuck!

(**TOM** *turns on his heel and marches determinedly through the kitchen and out the back door leading into the yard, where he stands, looking around in an unfocused panic. Then he sees the dustbin.*)

(*He rushes over, lifts up the dustbin lid, pulls out the gun from the holster, throws it into the bin, and walks away.*)

(*Then, almost instantly, he changes his mind. He rushes back and reaches into the bin to retrieve the gun. He's groping around in the bin when* **JINNY** *walks out through the back door.*)

(**TOM** *grabs the gun, shoves it behind his back, and rapidly freezes into an artificially casual pose.*)

(**JINNY** *stares at him.*)

Air. Needed some air.

(*He breathes exaggeratedly.*)

JINNY. Yes. Yes. Me too.

(They each stand silently for a moment, JINNY staring with a puzzled expression at TOM's rigid pose. A helicopter hovers somewhere overhead.)

JINNY. What is it you do, again, Tom?

TOM. Work in finance.

(TOM spits out his chewing gum.)

JINNY. Oh. Yes.

(They stand in silence again.)

Feeling okay?

TOM. Grand. Good. You?

JINNY. Sick, actually...

(JINNY gags, turns, and rushes back toward the bathroom.)

(In the living room, JANET is still crouching in front of BILL, who continues to avoid her gaze.)

JANET. *(Whispering.)* Is this true? Really, Bill? I'm so sorry. Oh god.

(She starts to cry. Coughs. Tries to control herself. MARTHA places a hand on her shoulders reassuringly. JANET looks up gratefully.)

MARTHA. Slow down. Slow down.

JANET. Yes. Yes.

MARTHA. Let's get practical. Bill.

BILL. Yes?

MARTHA. Who have you seen?

BILL. Harley Street specialist.

(JANET sits back on her heels abruptly.)

JANET. Hang on, hang on. You went private? You saw a private doctor?

BILL. I did.

JANET. You didn't try to get a referral from our GP?

BILL. Our GP couldn't see me for two bloody weeks.

JANET. Oh Christ.

> (**JANET** *puts her head in her hands as* **APRIL** *advances on* **BILL**.)

APRIL. What do you expect, Bill? Special treatment? Queue jumping? This is England! You can't make an exception for the husband of the minister. *Especially* not for the husband of the minister of health.

> (**JANET**'s *phone rings again. She bends down to pick it up off the carpet and turns away, glancing at the screen.*)

JANET. Shadow minister. But anyway, who cares?

APRIL. You do.

JANET. No. No, April. This is Bill. We must do anything we have to. Anything. It doesn't matter.

> (**APRIL** *looks at her incredulously.*)

APRIL. It's only your *principles*.

> (**JINNY** *re-appears in the doorway, conspicuously wiping her mouth for* **MARTHA**'s *benefit, though* **MARTHA** *doesn't seem to notice.*)

BILL. *(Muttering.)* Specialist saw me straightaway. All the tests. Done. Just like that.

JANET. And he's sure, it's definite?

BILL. Definite. He said I'm definitely done for.

> (**GOTTFRIED** *suddenly stands up very straight and speaks in a loud, clear voice:*)

GOTTFRIED. Western medicine is voodoo, Bill.

JINNY. Voodoo?

GOTTFRIED. *Voodoo.*

JINNY. Hey. I am with child –

APRIL. – Children, plural, wasn't it?

JINNY. – Yes *children*, thanks *entirely* to Western medicine.

MARTHA. Extremely Western. Extremely private. And extremely expensive.

JINNY. And worth it! Worth every penny! It's not *all* bad, Gottfried. IVF is basically a miracle.

APRIL. And I thought it was a procedure involving a petri dish...

JINNY. Well they give you a load of hormones, which is not much fun, actually, and the whole thing can be pretty painful, but it's amazing that the procedure, as you put it, April, can result in new life, don't you think?

(**TOM** *is pacing about restlessly in the hallway.*)

(**JANET** *looks around the room at her friends' distracted faces.*)

JANET. (*Quietly.*) Please. All of you. Stop it. Bill says he's dying.

APRIL. Not yet.

BILL. Soon.

(**TOM** *dives into the bathroom again, shuts the door behind him, and pulls out his wallet. He inhales deeply as another line of coke disappears up his nose. Then he collapses and lies down spread-eagled on the bathroom floor.*)

(*In the living room, it is now* **GOTTFRIED**'s *turn to kneel in front of* **BILL**.)

GOTTFRIED. Listen, Bill. Doctors are not prophets. They are cursing you with their so-called science, their so-called statistics.

Can they predict death? No. What do they really understand about illness? Nothing!

(**JANET** *sits down in a chair. She looks dazed.*)

MARTHA. Oh, come on Gottfried, you've gone too far. This is the land that invented the National Health Service. Free medical care for everyone! It changed the lives of millions for the better – and we are in the presence of one of its most passionate guardians.

(**MARTHA** *gestures toward* **JANET** *respectfully.*)

(**JANET**'s *phone pings. A text message. She picks up the phone and looks at the screen. [If the text message can be projected, it reads: "Missing you. xx." If not, we understand from her body language that it's an intimate message.]*)

(*She turns the phone facedown, glancing up to see if anyone noticed. Apparently not. They all seem to be listening to* **GOTTFRIED**.)

(*She sits very still, lost in her own thoughts.*)

GOTTFRIED. But – with respect – what exactly is she guarding? These so-called doctors do not look at the whole man when he is suffering. They see an illness, a collection of symptoms.

(**JANET** *suddenly picks up her phone again and decisively types a message. [If visible, it reads: "Bill ill. You and me over."]*)

(**GOTTFRIED** *rises to his feet.*)

(*In the bathroom,* **TOM** *also rises to his feet.*)

Then they try to eliminate the symptoms of this "disease" with poisonous chemicals sold by pharmaceutical companies that want to make money – only money.

(**TOM** *re-appears restlessly in the doorway, wide-eyed and over-alert.*)

TOM. (*Muttering.*) Yes, yes. Money. And why not? Why not?

(**GOTTFRIED** *turns to him.*)

GOTTFRIED. Because it is immoral to profit from the suffering of others. The Western medical establishment is ignorant and corrupt!

(**JANET**'s *phone pings again. She picks it up to read the incoming message. [It reads: "Never. Can't live without you. X."] She places her hand on her heart.*)

They are killing people with their so-called cures!

APRIL. Janet, I apologize for my "so-called" boyfriend. I cannot tolerate dogma, even when it's partially true.

GOTTFRIED. But it's *totally* true.

(**APRIL** *turns toward* **JANET.**)

APRIL. You can see why I am separating, definitively, from this...German.

(*But* **JANET** *is lost in reverie.*)

TOM. What the fuck does his nationality have to do with it?

(**APRIL** *gets up and crosses the room to stand next to* **GOTTFRIED** *as she answers Tom's question.*)

APRIL. Everything, when you know what the Nazis did with medical ethics.

GOTTFRIED. I am not a Nazi!

APRIL. You're very attached to dogma.

GOTTFRIED. I am working on my attachments.

APRIL. Work? You call that work?

(**GOTTFRIED** *raises his fist at* **APRIL** *in mock anger.*)

You see? Tickle an aromatherapist and you find a fascist.

GOTTFRIED. I am not an aromatherapist. I am a life coach... and healer.

(**GOTTFRIED** *looks down at* **BILL** *with a kindly expression.*)

MARTHA. Oh look. Let's face it, when you're in a car crash you don't want a life coach, you want an ambulance. But even so, April, I really think you should not use a word like Nazi as a form of abuse on the second generation. We are not responsible for the sins of our parents.

APRIL. Sin? You actually believe in sin, Martha? How very Christian of you. I mistakenly thought you were one of those atheists, always arguing with a god you don't believe in, just in case he's listening.

JINNY. She does argue a lot, actually. Mostly with me though.

> (**MARTHA** *glances crossly at* **JINNY.**)
>
> (**JANET** *emerges from her reverie.*)

JANET. Please. Stop it, right now. All of you. This is about Bill. *Bill.*

> (**TOM** *leaves the room and heads for the kitchen, where he paces about restlessly.*)
>
> (*In the living room,* **JANET** *rises to her feet and starts pacing back and forth across the carpet.*)

The man who stood by me through everything, who gave up a professorship at Harvard –

BILL & MARTHA. – Yale –

JANET. – Yale. Yes, of course. Yale. In order to support *me*. So I could fulfill *my* purpose. Here, in this country. Yes.

> (**JANET** *is talking in a low, empty voice as if she is on autopilot.*)

By doing all in my power to save our wonderful Health Service from its rampant destruction by those who are stealthily selling it off in lots to the highest bidder, turning it into a free-market corporate business opportunity.

> (**BILL** *is mouthing the familiar words along with her.*)

The ultimate consequence? Back to the nineteenth century, leaving the wretched poor to fend for themselves when they fall ill, whilst the rich can buy... can buy...

> (**JANET** *trails to a halt in mid-flow when she sees that* **BILL** *is mumbling her words in unison. She freezes.*)
>
> (*In the kitchen,* **TOM** *stops moving then sits down at the table.*)

*(In the living room, **JANET** throws herself forward and kneels down in front of **BILL**, clutching at him. He winces.)*

JANET. Oh, Bill, I'm so sorry. Why didn't I notice? Why didn't I see that you were ill? Please Bill. Look at me. Say something.

*(But **BILL** continues to ignore her in a long moment of silence.)*

JINNY. *(Stage whisper.)* Don't you think we should leave them alone for a minute?

APRIL. What for?

JINNY. Personal space?

GOTTFRIED. Right now, they need us. They need our attention.

MARTHA. What they need is our *friendship*. And some clear thinking.

JINNY. It was only a suggestion.

*(**GOTTFRIED** suddenly looks in the direction of the kitchen and sniffs.)*

GOTTFRIED. Burning. I smell burning.

*(**JANET** claps her hand to her mouth.)*

JANET. Oh, it's the vol-au-vents!

MARTHA. I'll deal with it.

APRIL. Isn't Jinny the chef?

MARTHA. A very good one, actually. Runner-up on *MasterChef* last year. Did you watch it?

APRIL. Two smears of parsnip and a grape coulis. How could I forget?

*(**APRIL** looks at **JINNY** pointedly.)*

So, Jinny, could you? Ten pounds. You have gained at least ten pounds, Martha, since the extremely touching ceremony. And oh! The matching hats...

*(**JINNY** sighs angrily and leaves the room.)*

(In the kitchen, **TOM** *is sitting at the table in the semi-dark as the room slowly fills with smoke.* **JINNY** *walks in, throws off her jacket, rolls up her sleeves, bends down, and opens the glowing oven door. Smoke billows out and she hurriedly slams it shut.)*

*(***JINNY*** looks around at* **TOM**.*)*

JINNY. Hey, you. Don't just sit there.

TOM. What can I do?

JINNY. Help me?

TOM. I cannot help anyone. I cannot help *myself*. I am burning.

JINNY. It's the pastry cases that are burning, Tom. Can you close the door and turn on the light, please?

*(***TOM*** gets up abruptly, turns on the light, and slams the kitchen door.)*

(In the living room, **BILL** *slowly looks up and meets* **GOTTFRIED**'s eyes.)*

BILL. Gottfried, do you think...

GOTTFRIED. Yes, my friend?

APRIL. Friend? Since when?

BILL. Do you *really* think that a terminal prognosis is a form of curse?

GOTTFRIED. Yes, I do.

BILL. You see, I am a materialist. And an atheist. My world view has been formed by reason and observation. Cause and effect. Logic and deduction. I have always been a rationalist, haven't I, Martha?

*(***BILL*** turns toward* **MARTHA**, *who is gazing at him fondly. She nods in agreement.)*

MARTHA. You have, Bill.

BILL. And from a statistical point of view, as Janet has so very often reminded me, it's your class background and economic status that will determine your general health and expected life span, infinitely more than diet or exercise.

(**JANET** *touches* **BILL***'s knee in a self-conscious gesture of solidarity.*)

JANET. Yes. That's why health is a political issue. We've always agreed about that, haven't we, Bill?

(**BILL** *ignores her, brushing her hand away from his knee.*)

BILL. So words like "curse" and "voodoo" have never really featured in my vocabulary. But now...everything looks different.

GOTTFRIED. *(Gently.)* Perhaps everything *is* different.

BILL. Maybe it is. But the worst of it is this: I am asking myself an unanswerable question, even a *metaphysical* question.

(**JANET** *looks up at him, puzzled.*)

GOTTFRIED. What question is that, my friend?

(**BILL** *struggles to answer.*)

BILL. *Why me?*

(**GOTTFRIED** *moves closer to* **BILL** *and speaks in a low, confiding voice:*)

GOTTFRIED. When a person becomes sick, there is always a reason. If not in this life, then in a past life...

(**JANET** *gives up and lies down despairingly on the carpet.*)

APRIL. Gottfried, you are an embarrassment.

MARTHA. Possibly, but at least he's trying to help.

APRIL. You're defending Gottfried now?

MARTHA. April, I too am frequently described by internet trolls as an embarrassment. Or worse. Much worse, actually. Is it a crime to be an embarrassment?

APRIL. Martha, you are a first-class lesbian, but a second-rate thinker. Must be all those women's studies.

MARTHA. April, really. I am a professor, specializing in domestic labor gender differentiation in American Utopianism.

APRIL. My point exactly.

> (*In the kitchen, the smoke alarm starts shrieking piercingly.* **JINNY** *is trying to flap the smoke out of the kitchen door with a cloth.*)

JINNY. Do something, Tom!

TOM. What? What can I do?

JINNY. Turn that thing off! Or pull it off, or something.

> (**TOM** *clambers onto the table and stares up at the alarm, covering his ears.* **JINNY** *stares up at him.*)

You're really sweaty.

TOM. I told you, I am burning.

> (**TOM** *presses the button on the alarm repeatedly and uselessly. He's in a panic.*)

JINNY. Hey. Are you ill too? Is it contagious? Because I'm pregnant, you see. Triplets, actually.

TOM. So I gather.

JINNY. I have to protect my babies.

> (**TOM** *looks down at* **JINNY.**)

TOM. Yes, you do have to protect your babies. Like I have to protect my marriage. Understand?

> (**JINNY** *stares up at him, puzzled.*)

JINNY. Yes...maybe...

TOM. You are fortunate, you see, Jinny. Myself and Marianne, we have not had any babies.

JINNY. Right. Neither has anyone else at this party, as far as I know. So you're definitely not ill, then?

> (**TOM** *bends down toward her, gesturing dramatically.*)

TOM. It is not *me* who is sick. *Sick.*

> (**JINNY** *stares up at* **TOM** *through the swirling smoke.*)

JINNY. Then why aren't you turning that thing off?

MARTHA. *(Shouting from the living room.)* Jinny, are you doing all right in there?

> *(**JINNY** pulls the tray of smoldering pastry cases out of the oven.)*

JINNY. *(Shouting, irritated.)* Yes, I'm *fine*, thanks. *Tom's* helping me, *thank* you.

> *(**TOM** picks up a roll of foil and repeatedly bashes the alarm until it crashes to the floor.)*

> *(**JINNY** stares up at him in the sudden silence.)*

Look. Can I ask you something? Did I see you out there...before... I mean, were you getting something out of the...

> *(But **TOM** jumps down from the table, ignoring her question.)*

> *(In the increasingly shadowy living room, **APRIL** gets up, crosses the room, and kneels down next to **JANET** in front of **BILL**.)*

APRIL. Right. Now that infernal shrieking has stopped, let's get to the point. Listen, Bill, have they suggested chopping a few bits out? Or off?

> *(**JANET** groans. **BILL** looks at **APRIL**. **GOTTFRIED** looks at **BILL**.)*

Because if they have, I think you should seriously consider it. What do you say, Gottfried? Surgery, a good choice for Bill, yes or no, from a life-coach standpoint?

> *(**GOTTFRIED** looks at **APRIL** thoughtfully.)*

GOTTFRIED. *(Gently.)* Despite my criticisms of most modern medicine, I believe surgery can sometimes be healing, April, as you know. Karmically cleansing.

> *(**JANET** and **APRIL** both take a deep breath.)*

APRIL. Right. Won't argue, because Janet doesn't want me to, but you are full of shit about karma. Though surprisingly good on the knife question.

(**JINNY** *suddenly appears in the doorway, carrying the tray of smoking vol-au-vent pastry cases. It's getting seriously dark by now, and no one has bothered to turn on the overhead lights.*)

JINNY. Martha! I need to talk to you. Where are you? I can hardly see anything in here. And I'm starting to feel really queasy again!

(*She drops the tray – which lies smouldering on the floor – and rushes toward the bathroom.* **MARTHA** *glances up in Jinny's direction and hesitates, but does not immediately follow her.*)

GOTTFRIED. It's probably because she's pregnant.

APRIL. Genius.

(**JINNY** *rushes into the bathroom, slamming the door behind her. She lifts the lavatory seat and vomits noisily into the lavatory bowl.* **TOM** *stands outside the bathroom door, listening to* **JINNY** *retching. He hesitates then knocks on the door.*)

TOM. Jinny? Are you all right?

(**JINNY** *wipes her mouth and looks up in the direction of the bathroom door.*)

JINNY. No. I'm not. Where's Martha?

TOM. In the other room. She's in there with *him*.

JINNY. Well, could you tell her to come *here*?

TOM. What for?

JINNY. Because she's my wife! And I'm being sick! And I think she should be looking after me, actually. Don't you?

(**TOM** *looks agitated and distracted as he peers into the living room then turns back and hovers outside the bathroom door again.*)

TOM. Don't I what?

JINNY. Oh never mind. Just go and fetch her, will you? I want to say something to her.

(**TOM** *freezes, suddenly looking more focused.*)

TOM. Jinny. Listen. You need to tell me what it is that you want to say to Martha. Okay? I need to know what it is. Is there something you have to say about *me*?

(**JINNY** *sits down on the floor next to the lavatory and stares at the door silently.*)

Is there something that you think you *saw*?

JINNY. Maybe. What do *you* think I want to say to her about you? What do *you* think I saw?

(**TOM** *seems uncertain what to say. Or do.*)

(*In the living room,* **GOTTFRIED** *is sitting on the floor next to* **BILL**.)

BILL. Knowledge, Gottfried.

GOTTFRIED. Yes?

BILL. Is mutable.

(**GOTTFRIED** *nods sagely.*)

And culturally specific.

MARTHA. True, but where's this line of thought heading, chum?

(**BILL** *turns to look at* **MARTHA**.)

BILL. Well maybe Gottfried has a point. What once seemed like medical science, now looks like superstition, does it not, Martha? Leeches, purging, blood-letting and so on? There's no universal agreement about the causes of illness. And certainly no historically consistent ideas about what constitutes a cure.

JANET. There are some baseline principles.

(**BILL** *ignores her.*)

BILL. And then there is the mystery of the placebo effect...

GOTTFRIED. The so-called mystery of the placebo effect is, in fact, proof of the innate ability of the body to heal itself.

APRIL. Wish I didn't agree with your analysis.

> (**GOTTFRIED** *turns to her with a triumphant grin.*)

GOTTFRIED. But you do, my darling.

BILL. So what have you found, Gottfried? With your...er... healing thing? Do you think... That is to say...

> (**JANET** *stares at* **BILL** *intently.* **BILL** *seems to be steeling himself to ask a difficult question.*)

Can *faith* do it?

APRIL & MARTHA. *Faith? You?*

> (**GOTTFRIED** *looks up at them sternly.*)

GOTTFRIED. And why not? Bill is growing extraordinarily fast, from a spiritual point of view.

APRIL. There you are. As soon as I reluctantly agree with one of your wretched ideas, you go and ruin it.

> (**JINNY** *is still retching audibly in the lavatory.* **MARTHA** *inches toward the door with a guilty expression but can't leave this alone.*)

MARTHA. Concerning spirituality, Gottfried, Bill has debated with leading rabbis, bishops, and imams and *won.* He's even written a book about it. *Reason, Roads, and Religion.*

> (**MARTHA** *turns decisively to leave the room, but* **TOM** *suddenly appears, blocking her exit.*)

TOM. Roads? Is there a connection, Martha? Between roads and religion?

MARTHA. *(Crisply.)* Bill specialized in Roman history, Tom, as I think you know – didn't he supervise Marianne's PhD?

TOM. Yes, he did, he did supervise her PhD, her fucking PhD –

MARTHA. – And roads link more than cities. They also link ideas.

TOM. Well, thank you Martha. Thank you for illuminating me on the question of *roads*.

> (**MARTHA** *leaves the room and heads toward the bathroom, where she hovers outside the door.*)

JANET. Please! The only road that matters now is the road to Bill's recovery.

> (*But* **BILL** *is ignoring her. It seems he is only interested in* **GOTTFRIED**. *Their heads are almost touching.*)

BILL. Do you believe in recovery, Gottfried?

GOTTFRIED. I do.

BILL. Even in a case like mine?

GOTTFRIED. I do.

BILL. So you think I have a future?

GOTTFRIED. *(Gently.)* As surely as you had a past.

APRIL. Isn't this going too far? Gottfried may have his good points but is not, repeat *not* a guru.

> (*In the hallway,* **MARTHA** *is knocking on the bathroom door. No response.*)

MARTHA. Jin. Are you all right?

> (*The lavatory flushes, and* **JINNY** *eventually opens the door.*)

JINNY. No, I'm absolutely not. Apart from the vomiting, which is vile, my least favorite thing – and if it continues like this my pregnancy will be a *nightmare* – I'm a little bit concerned about Tom.

MARTHA. Tom? Why worry about *him*?

> (**JINNY** *gestures and* **MARTHA** *turns to look into the living room, where* **TOM** *is clenching and unclenching his fists as he stares at* **BILL** *and* **GOTTFRIED**.)

> (**GOTTFRIED** *has wrapped his arm round* **BILL**'s *shoulders and is speaking to him in a low, intimate tone of voice:*)

GOTTFRIED. Listen, my friend.

APRIL. Again. The mystery deepens.

GOTTFRIED. It *is* a mystery. But the truth is also very simple. You just have to listen to the voice within. If you seek, you will find...

APRIL. *(Groaning.)* Jesus.

> (**TOM** *suddenly steps forward and switches on the ceiling light, which is hanging immediately above Bill's head.*)
>
> (**BILL** *looks up, blinking fearfully in the sudden harsh brightness.*)

TOM. Since we're talking about truth, Bill, is there something you might want to add? I think you know what I'm talking about, Bill. Truth. Truth! Is that a concept any of you have heard of?

> (*The others turn toward* **TOM**, *surprised by his aggressive tone.*)
>
> (**JANET** *looks bewildered. She stares at* **TOM** *then at* **BILL**, *who is silent and sitting very still.*)
>
> (**MARTHA** *steps toward* **TOM** *and touches his arm.*)

MARTHA. Tom. Let's step outside for a moment –

> (*But* **TOM** *brushes her away.*)

TOM. No, Martha, no.

BILL. *(Softly.)* Yes, I do. Yes. I do have something to add, Tom.

> (**BILL** *turns and looks up at* **JANET**. *As their eyes meet, her face shows surprise and relief at the connection. She kneels in front of him and puts her hand on his knee.*)

JANET. What is it darling?

BILL. I'm sorry, Janet. This is it. I'm leaving you.

> (**JANET** *gazes up at him.*)

JANET. No! We'll beat this! Together. I'll be by your side.

TOM. No, Janet. I think he means he's leaving you...in a different sense.

MARTHA. *(Muttering.)* Tom, come on. That's enough.

TOM. No! Martha! It's not.

>   *(**JANET** looks up at them, bewildered.)*

JANET. What's going on?

TOM. Come on, Bill. Just tell her. What have you got to lose? Huh?

>   *(**BILL** straightens up, looks **JANET** in the eye, and clears his throat.)*

BILL. Whatever time I have left, Janet – which it seems is debatable, depending on your point of view – I intend to spend –

JANET. – Together, we'll be together –

BILL. – In the company of...of another woman.

>   *(**JANET** looks confused. She laughs nervously.)*

JANET. What on earth are you talking about? Another woman. What other woman?

>   *(There's a long, awkward pause. Everyone in the room has frozen.)*

Bill?

>   *(Silence.)*

What are you saying exactly, Bill?

>   *(**BILL** lowers his gaze slowly.)*

What other woman?

>   *(Still no answer.)*

Who?

>   *(**JANET** rises to her feet. She stares down at **BILL**. She's suddenly on high alert.)*

(Shouting.) Who?

>   *(**BILL** slowly lifts his head and stares at her.)*

BILL. *(Quietly.)* Marianne.

> *(**JANET** freezes.)*

JANET. *(Softly.)* Marianne?

> *(**APRIL** steps forward with a face like thunder.)*

APRIL. The lovely Marianne? With *you*, Bill?

> *(**JANET** still hasn't moved.)*
>
> *(She stares at **BILL** with an expression of confusion and rage. Then she lunges forward and hits **BILL** wildly. He collapses to one side, clutching the side of his face.)*

Fuck.

> *(**JANET** pulls back, horrified, when she sees that blood is starting to trickle down **BILL**'s chin from a cut on his lip. She scrambles backward. Sits on the nearest chair. Sits on her hands.)*

JANET. What am I doing? I don't do this.

APRIL. You just did.

JANET. No! This isn't me. I shouldn't have hit you. I shouldn't have hurt you... I'm sorry. I'm so sorry.

> *(But then it rises up in her again. The uncontrollable heat of sheer rage.)*

(Shouting.) But I could kill you!

> *(She gets up, rushes toward **BILL**, and lashes out again, hitting the other side of his face.)*
>
> *(**BILL** touches the blood now oozing out of a cut above his eye.)*

Why? Just tell me why. Why now? Of all days? And why...*her*?

> *(**JANET** looks around the room wildly then turns to **APRIL** pleadingly.)*

Stop me! April, stop me from hurting Bill!

APRIL. What for?

JANET. Because he's sick. He's dying.

APRIL. Debatable, according to Gottfried.

TOM. *(Coolly.)* Why don't you tell Janet how long you've been sleeping with my wife, Bill?

> (**TOM** *grabs a bottle of champagne and gestures at* **MARTHA** *accusingly.*)

Or Martha, perhaps *you* would like to inform Janet, as I believe that you have, on occasion, lent your attractive shabby-chic femme-nest apartment to your good old pal Bill. Isn't that right? Huh?

> (**JANET** *turns to* **MARTHA** *with a horrified expression.*)

JANET. Martha. You knew?

APRIL. Sounds like she was an accomplice in this heinous crime. Well, what a surprise, professor.

JANET. Marianne! And Bill? In your flat, Martha?

> (**MARTHA**'s *mouth moves silently. She can't bring herself to say it.*)

BILL. Yes.

> (**JANET** *wheels back to face him.*)

JANET. For how long?

BILL. *(Hesitantly.)* A year.

JANET. *(Whispering.)* A year?

TOM. A fucking year?

BILL. Well, two. Or so.

TOM. *What?*

JANET. The whole time? During the campaign? While I was on the road? And we spoke every night on the phone and you kept telling me I could do it?

BILL. You *did* do it.

JANET. And you were doing it – with Marianne – in Martha's flat – while I did it?

> (**JANET** *turns back to* **MARTHA**.)

I thought you were a friend. I thought you were a *sister*.

APRIL. That dates you, Janet. Sisterhood is a very aging concept, sweetheart.

MARTHA. *(Quietly.)* I do consider myself your friend. And I really thought about saying something. But...

JANET. But what?

MARTHA. You were so...busy.

JANET. Yes. I *was* busy! Incredibly busy!

TOM. *(Muttering.)* They always say they're busy.

JANET. I was working day and night for the party! For *our* party. Yes, Martha. I was working for all of us! Why didn't you just *tell* me?

MARTHA. You didn't seem to want to know. About anything except politics.

> *(**JANET** stares at her for a moment, incredulous as she takes this in.)*

JANET. And because I was so dedicated to saving our country from profiteering butchery you decided to let them do it in your flat?

MARTHA. *(Quietly.)* I thought better than in your house. From your point of view.

JANET. *(Bitterly.)* Yeah, well, that's some kind of friendship.

BILL. She was *my* friend first.

> *(**JANET** wheels back around to look at **BILL**, who seems to have recovered some of his energy and sobriety despite – or perhaps because of – the cut above his eye and the split lip, which he is feeling with his fingertips appreciatively. He looks younger, suddenly. Almost boyish.)*
>
> *(He puts another record on the turntable.)*

[MUSIC CUE 7]

> *(A slow, sensuous instrumental arrangement of a love song.)*

We shared a house at University. In fact...we shared everything.

APRIL. Everything?

> (**JINNY** *steps forward and looks at* **MARTHA**, *deep furrows appearing suddenly in her brow.*)

JINNY. *Everything?*

JANET. Oh Jinny! What about you? Did you know too?

JINNY. Only a little bit.

JANET. What, like being "a little bit" pregnant?

> (**JANET** *advances toward* **MARTHA** *and* **JINNY** *angrily.*)

> (**JINNY** *grabs* **MARTHA**, *pulling her across the room toward the French doors leading out into the backyard.*)

JINNY. Look, Martha, don't you think we should be going? This is getting very *physical* and...what *exactly* did you "share" with Bill at University?

MARTHA. *(Quietly.)* A house. Digs. For God's sake...don't start.

JINNY. Don't talk to me like that. I am a woman with child, Martha –

APRIL. – Children. Three.

JINNY. Yes, three. Triplets. One, two, three.

MARTHA. I can count. And – by the way – you could have waited 'til we got home before you told me.

JINNY. You could have come to the scan. You *should* have come to the scan. You're so unsupportive, Martha.

> (**JINNY** *walks away furiously into the yard.*)

MARTHA. That is not true. I've been to nearly every support group.

> (**JINNY** *turns and walks back to* **MARTHA**. *They're both shouting now.*)

JINNY. One. And there have been three. Which makes two –

MARTHA. – I can count, as I just mentioned.

JINNY. Don't patronize me! And you still haven't answered my question. What else did you share with Bill?

MARTHA. Stop this!

JANET. *(Bitterly.)* So you both knew. Right. Who else knew? April? Did you know too?

APRIL. No. I did not. Although I expect the worst of everyone – in the name of realism – I was too preoccupied with Gottfried's screamingly obvious faults to notice this unfolding drama.

BILL. Why should *you* have noticed? Janet didn't. In fact she hasn't noticed anything about me for years.

> (**JANET** *looks at him, devastated.*)

JANET. *(Quietly.)* How can you say that?

BILL. Because now I know what it feels like when someone *does* notice. And likes what they see. A *lot*.

> (**TOM** *sits down heavily, trembling.* **JINNY** *covers her face as* **JANET** *rushes toward* **BILL** *again, lashing out with her fists.* **BILL** *lifts his arms ineffectively, barely trying to protect himself from her blows. Or perhaps he is deliberately allowing them to rain down on him.*)

Go on. Do it. Do it! At least it shows you're capable of some passion!

JANET. What's happening to me?

APRIL. Revenge.

JANET. No. No. I don't believe in revenge. I never have! I've given speeches about it. All over the world. Truth and reconciliation! I believe in truth and reconciliation.

> (**JANET** *collapses on the sofa, biting her hand, screaming and weeping with shame.* **TOM** *lowers his head into his hands despairingly.*)

APRIL. Reconciliation comes a bit later. If at all, in my experience.

(**TOM** *suddenly gets up and strides through the kitchen into the yard, unbuttoning his jacket.*)

(*He pulls the gun out of the holster, opens the dustbin lid, and, after wiping the gun with his handkerchief, chucks it decisively into the bin. Then he heads back through the kitchen toward the living room, where he sits down again, quietly, at the back of the room.*)

(**GOTTFRIED** *is gently pulling* **JANET**'s *hand away from her mouth. He looks at her kindly.*)

GOTTFRIED. I believe it is better to hit a cushion than to eat yourself.

APRIL. A cushion! She wants to smash his face in, not ruin her soft furnishings.

GOTTFRIED. You need to let the anger out, Janet. It's only natural.

JINNY. Yes, that's how I feel. I'd like to let some anger out, too.

(**JINNY** *looks at* **MARTHA** *coldly.*)

What else did you share with Bill? Exactly?

MARTHA. I already told you.

JINNY. No. You never told me about Bill.

MARTHA. He was my best friend at University, you know that.

JINNY. What kind of best friend? Did you sleep together?

(**BILL** *laughs merrily.*)

BILL. Once. Or twice. It was a mistake. I think we agreed about that at the time, didn't we Martha? It was fun, though.

JANET. *(Groaning.)* Oh no. No.

(**JANET** *staggers out of the room, tripping over the smouldering tray of blackened vol-au-vents.*)

JINNY. So you *have* had a man inside you, after all. And it was *fun*? That's so disgusting! I'm disgusted!

> *(She turns and stomps out into the yard.)*

APRIL. Sounds like you might have *three* little men inside *you*.

> *(And now it's* **TOM** *who laughs, bitterly, sitting alone in his chair at the far end of the room.)*

> *(In the kitchen,* **JANET** *hesitates then – as if on autopilot – picks up a cloth and turns back into the living room to pick up the smouldering tray from the floor. She walks through the kitchen into the yard, balances the tray with one hand, lifts the dustbin lid with the other, then turns the tray upside down and shakes it violently.)*

> *(The burnt pastries are stuck to the tray. She shakes it again, more violently.)*

> *(Something catches her eye.)*

> *(***JANET*** reaches slowly into the bin.)*

> *(She gingerly pulls out the gun, brushing off the blackened flakes of pastry. Then, in a sudden impulse, she wraps it in the cloth and runs back through the kitchen, along the hallway, then into the bathroom, where she locks the door.)*

> *(She sits down on the lavatory seat and tentatively unwraps the cloth to reveal the gun then stares at it for a long, quiet moment.)*

> *(In the living room,* **BILL** *puts on a new record.)*

[MUSIC CUE 8]

> *(Slow, relaxing reggae.)*

> *(***APRIL*** stretches out on the sofa, exhausted.)*

(**BILL** *turns to look at* **GOTTFRIED**, *who is watching him from the middle of the room, smiling.*)

GOTTFRIED. It's good. It's good that this is all coming out. Very good.

(**BILL** *walks toward* **GOTTFRIED**.)

But now I think you need to protect yourself from so much negative female energy.

(**BILL** *nods affirmatively.* **APRIL** *sits up abruptly.*)

APRIL. Gottfried, you are surpassing yourself.

(**BILL** *ignores* **APRIL**. *He only has eyes for* **GOTTFRIED**.)

BILL. How? How do I do that?

GOTTFRIED. I will help you.

(**APRIL** *stalks out of the room then stops by the door and turns around to glower at* **BILL**.)

APRIL. I seem to remember, Bill, that you called yourself a feminist. In the old days.

BILL. Everything has changed.

GOTTFRIED. Change is good.

TOM. Why is change good?

(**GOTTFRIED** *gestures with a kindly expression toward* **TOM**, *who is still sitting at the far end of the room.*)

GOTTFRIED. Tom. Come. Sit. Try to relax a little.

(**TOM** *stays put.*)

(*In the bathroom,* **JANET**'s *phone rings. She picks it up automatically, her face forming into a habitual rictus of polite friendliness. But her voice is flat. Empty.*)

JANET. It's very kind of you to call. Yes, we're having a little celebration. Well, I must agree, it has been quite a journey.

(**APRIL** *knocks at the bathroom door.*)

Thanks so much. Absolutely. Looking forward to it. I'll see you tomorrow. First thing. Can't wait.

(**JANET** *throws her phone violently onto the bathroom floor, where it shatters.* **APRIL** *knocks on the door again.*)

APRIL. Janet. It's me. Come on. Let me in, darling.

(*Silence.*)

Listen to me. One of the reasons I have never believed in parliamentary politics is that the procedures are so slow. So bureaucratic. You can't always vote your way out of conflict.

(**JANET** *sits very still, listening to* **APRIL**'s *voice on the other side of the door.*)

Direct action, swift decisive moves, *that's* what gets things done.

(**JANET** *suddenly gets up, crosses the bathroom, lifts the lid of the laundry basket, and dumps the gun inside.*)

(**APRIL** *leans against the bathroom door and speaks to* **JANET** *in a clear, loving tone:*)

Remember when I used to be an idealist like you? All those marches we went on together, thinking someone in power would listen? Well, now I'm a realist. And I do believe, under the circumstances, that although it might have a deleterious effect on your career strategy, you could consider murder.

(**JANET** *gets up, opens the bathroom door, and falls into* **APRIL**'s *arms.*)

(*In the backyard,* **JINNY** *and* **MARTHA** *are sitting side by side on a bench.*)

JINNY. I just can't believe you slept with that hairy old man. That disgusting, randy old rapist!

MARTHA. It was over thirty years ago. It was nearly *forty* years ago. You were still in kindergarten at the time.

Bill used to help run the crèche at conferences, as a matter of fact.

JINNY. Oh, so maybe he should be my doula. Just to round things out.

MARTHA. By the way, he's not especially hairy. And furthermore, not all men are rapists. I really think we've moved beyond that position.

JINNY. What position? What are you talking about, Martha?

MARTHA. Men are not the enemy! That debate is over! It is finished!

> *(In the living room,* **TOM** *suddenly rushes toward* **BILL**, *brandishing a champagne bottle, roaring like a wounded beast, but then carries on past him and hurls the champagne bottle out into the yard where it shatters on the ground.)*

> *(***JINNY** *and* **MARTHA** *leap to their feet and run to safety.)*

> *(***GOTTFRIED** *puts his arm tenderly around* **TOM***'s shoulders and draws him back into the room.)*

GOTTFRIED. Tom, my friend. Now that you have expressed your feelings, let's put a stop to all this violence and talk together, as men. The three of us.

> *(***GOTTFRIED** *gently guides* **TOM** *to the sofa, continuing to touch him reassuringly.* **BILL** *watches them warily from his chair.)*

This is a crisis that can become a moment of deep personal transformation.

> *(***TOM** *turns to face* **GOTTFRIED***.)*

TOM. But I don't want to transform. I just want my wife back. Gottfried, I just want things to be the way they were before. Why do you people always want everything to change?

GOTTFRIED. Everything changes whether we want it to or not. We cannot fight impermanence.

TOM. I am not fighting fucking impermanence! I am fighting for the love of my *life*! For *life*!

> (**TOM**'s *hurt is really showing for the first time. He is shaking and tears are rolling down his cheeks.*)

BILL. So am I. Life! *Life!*

GOTTFRIED. This is good. You share an impulse.

TOM. I do not share *anything* with him, especially not...

GOTTFRIED. Tom, I think someone in your profession is perhaps not familiar with *losing*.

TOM. I never lose. Gottfried, I do not lose. I am... I am a winner. Do you understand? I am a *winner*.

GOTTFRIED. I also think you are in shock.

TOM. Yes. Yes.

GOTTFRIED. Tom, when exactly did you discover...

TOM. Today. I found out today.

BILL. She told you at last. Ah, Marianne. I knew you would.

TOM. She did not tell me. I read your texts and I read your fucking emails.

> (**TOM** *pulls out his phone and rapidly scrolls down.*)

Look at this, Gottfried. "Let us live and let us love..."

BILL. Catullus.

TOM. "Let us too give in to love..."

BILL. Virgil.

TOM. "You who seek an end to love...an end to love..."

> (**TOM** *gestures at the screen wildly.*)

"You who seek an end to love, love will yield to business"! What the fuck is that?

BILL. She wants love and ideas, you see, Tom, not money and business. Such an intelligent, such a sensitive woman. Such a *passionate* woman.

> (**TOM** *starts to get up, but* **GOTTFRIED** *gently restrains him.*)

GOTTFRIED. Brothers. You have something beautiful in common.

BILL. We have nothing in common.

GOTTFRIED. Oh, but you do. You both love Marianne. And love is a very powerful force.

BILL. Gottfried, you do realize that Tom is one of those amoral money men, strutting about in his city suit –

TOM. – Here we go. Oh, you fucking English intellectuals, you think you're so superior.

(**TOM** *rises to his feet.*)

(*Shouting.*) Even *you* need money, Bill! Money bought this house, not fucking ideas!

(*And now* **BILL** *is on his feet too.*)

BILL. Not with your dirty money!

TOM. No money is clean, Bill. It all comes through the system and into your pocket! Into your grubby little pocket!

BILL. But that's *real* money. Cash, Tom. You trade in fictional profits stolen from workers' hard-earned pension funds –

TOM. – Stolen! That's pretty fucking hypocritical from the mouth of the man that stole my wife! You stole my *wife*!

BILL. She *chose* me.

TOM. She did not choose you. She did not choose you. Not *you*. She can't have.

(**TOM** *waves dismissively at* **BILL**.)

BILL. But she did. She chose me. We're in love.

(**TOM** *rushes at* **BILL** *and hits him wildly, socking him on the jaw.* **BILL** *falls to the ground, out cold.*)

(*In the bathroom,* **JANET** *is sitting on the edge of the bath.* **APRIL** *is sticking an Elastoplast on* **JANET**'s *wounded knee.*)

JANET. I'm finished, April.

APRIL. Nonsense. Listen. I realize I risk sounding uncannily like Gottfried, but I believe what you are experiencing is a *feeling*.

JANET. It's a horrible feeling!

APRIL. I can see it's unpleasant. But like all feelings it will surely pass.

> (**JANET** *looks at* **APRIL** *then gets up and starts pacing about.*)

JANET. Have *you* ever felt like this, April? Split in two?

APRIL. Often.

JANET. Thought you wanted one thing and then found you wanted another?

APRIL. Frequently. But listen, Janet. You don't really want to resign, do you? After all these years of tedious effort to get to the so-called top? Please don't let Bill's entirely predictable infidelity sabotage your hard-earned success.

> (**JANET** *sits down next to* **APRIL** *on the edge of the bath.*)

Though, personally, I have always found success so stifling; another reason I can't share your desire for political power.

JANET. But it's not about power, April. It's about the possibility of...of doing good. I've spent my entire working life trying to put things right. For society as a whole, that is.

APRIL. That's very worthy of you, Janet. Though of course, if you'd been born working class in this country you'd have gone into politics out of sheer rage.

JANET. But I *am* angry. Very. About all the things that are wrong. About poverty. Discrimination. Injustice.

APRIL. And Bill.

> (*In the living room,* **BILL** *is still lying on the carpet, out cold.* **TOM** *and* **GOTTFRIED** *are now both bending over him.*)

TOM. Oh fuck. Fuck, fuck, fuck. Is he alive? Gottfried, tell me, is he alive?

(**GOTTFRIED** *is checking* **BILL***'s pulse, listening to his chest, hovering close to his impassive face and blank, staring eyes.*)

I'm so sorry! Oh Bill! I'm so sorry! Gottfried! What do we do now? What do we do?

(**TOM** *is frantic.* **GOTTFRIED** *looks up at him calmly.*)

GOTTFRIED. Just wait and see.

(**GOTTFRIED** *puts his ear close to* **BILL***'s mouth. Low, ominous gurgling sounds.*)

Ah. He is alive. Yes. He's alive.

TOM. I'll put on some music. Shall I? He likes music. Yes. I'll put on some music.

(**TOM** *scrambles to his feet and dashes wildly across the room toward Bill's sound system. He randomly selects a record, slams it onto the turntable, and lowers the needle.*)

[MUSIC CUE 9]

(*It's a slow, mournful arrangement.*)

(**GOTTFRIED** *slowly and tenderly strokes* **BILL***'s face and head.*)

(*In the backyard,* **JINNY** *is still sitting on the bench, softly weeping.* **MARTHA** *stares at her for a moment then pulls out a pack of cigarettes and heads toward the dustbins. She pulls out a cigarette and lights up, exhaling smoke in the darkness.*)

(*In the bathroom,* **APRIL** *is perched on the edge of the bath, gazing up at* **JANET***, who is now standing in front of her.*)

APRIL. I adore you, Janet. But if you really want to run this country – and we both know that you do – and, actually, you *must*, for all our sakes – you will have to do something about your hair.

(JANET stares at her.)

JANET. My hair? I'm a shadow minister April – well I was, earlier today – and you're talking about my hair?

APRIL. And your clothes, darling. Then you could have the *inner* beauty, all those terrific principles and so on, and at least a chance against the competition. And I'm referring to your political opponents, Janet, not the seemingly irresistible Marianne.

*(In the backyard, **JINNY** stands up, and **MARTHA** slowly walks toward her, moving in and out of shadows.)*

MARTHA. Did they tell you that they were boys?

JINNY. No, we agreed. We agreed not to know.

MARTHA. *(Tenderly.)* But did you see, on the screen? Their little legs, and toes…and things?

JINNY. No, I didn't want to look, and I felt sick.

MARTHA. But three boys? It's almost a football team.

JINNY. Don't you want them? Have you changed your mind?

MARTHA. I'm not sure my mind – or yours, for that matter, was involved in this decision. For a start, we'll have to move.

JINNY. What? From our lovely little nest?

MARTHA. Our place was designed for two, not five. It's just not practical.

*(In the living room, **BILL** still hasn't moved. **GOTTFRIED** looks up at **TOM** with a worried expression.)*

GOTTFRIED. Tom, this might be the wrong piece of music.

*(**TOM** nods, dashes back to the sound system, and randomly selects another record.)*

[MUSIC CUE 10]

(This time it is wild gypsy music.)

(**TOM** *runs back, lifts* **BILL**'s *limp arm, and moves it rhythmically in time to the beat.*)

TOM. Oh god. I'm so sorry. But it's going to be okay. Come on, Bill. It's going to be all right.

(*But* **TOM**'s *manic entreaties are going nowhere. He looks up at* **GOTTFRIED** *imploringly.*)

He is going to be okay? Isn't he? Gottfried?

(*In the bathroom, it's* **APRIL**'s *turn to sit on the lavatory seat and* **JANET**'s *turn to sit perched on the edge of the bath.*)

JANET. April.

APRIL. Janet.

JANET. We've known each other a long time. I want you to be truthful with me.

APRIL. Have I ever been anything else?

JANET. Well, you disguise yourself as a cynic.

APRIL. Everyone is in disguise. Including you. All that fake political certainty.

JANET. It's not fake. It's just that sometimes you have to pretend. In order to win.

APRIL. Well, it hasn't worked for your party for a while and it wont work for you.

(**JANET** *looks at* **APRIL**. *It seems as if she is about to say something, but she stops herself and turns her head away.*)

(*Tenderly.*) You're lost aren't you, Janet? Incredibly competent. But lost.

(*In the backyard,* **MARTHA** *and* **JINNY** *are standing facing each other. When* **MARTHA** *moves closer, a security light clicks on.*)

MARTHA. I have to think.

JINNY. Don't think! It might ruin everything. It usually does.

MARTHA. Well someone has to do the thinking, especially now that you're taking care of the animal side of things.

(JINNY stares at her, incredulous.)

JINNY. Animal! Is that what you think I've become? A few more hormones flying around my body to support new life and suddenly I'm an *animal*?

> *(MARTHA shrugs and answers as if on autopilot.)*

MARTHA. The reproductive instinct *is* part of the reptilian brain.

JINNY. So now you're calling me a *reptile*?

> *(The security light clicks off and the two women are once more standing in the dark.)*
>
> *(In the living room, TOM changes the record again.)*

[MUSIC CUE 11]

> *(This time it's beautiful, melancholic Portuguese guitar.)*
>
> *(TOM gestures questioningly at GOTTFRIED.)*

TOM. This? Gottfried?

> *(GOTTFRIED looks at TOM and moves his head in time to the music but cannot answer. He now looks seriously worried.)*
>
> *(In the backyard, JINNY walks away from MARTHA then stops, turns on her heel, and faces MARTHA again.)*

JINNY. Martha, after this evening I never want to see you again. I'm going to do this on my own.

MARTHA. Don't be ridiculous.

JINNY. I would rather give birth alone than with you, if this is what you really think of me. After everything you said. Have you forgotten our beautiful vows, Martha?

> *(JINNY stares at MARTHA, who is hovering mutely.)*

It's over, isn't it? We're through.

(And then it comes out. **MARTHA***'s voice softens:)*

MARTHA. *(Softly.)* I'm just afraid, Jinny. That's all. Just afraid. I'm afraid of losing everything that we had. I'm afraid of losing each other. And I'm afraid of losing you...to our sons.

*(***MARTHA*** moves closer to* **JINNY** *and reaches out to her, tenderly.)*

Please don't leave me. I love you more than life itself.

(In the living room, **BILL** *still hasn't moved.* **TOM** *keeps trying to rouse him, hopelessly.)*

TOM. Come on. Bill. Please. Come on! Come on!

*(***TOM*** looks distraught. He lies down next to* **BILL** *on the carpet, cradling* **BILL***'s head gently.)*

Bill! Bill...

*(***TOM*** puts his arm around* **BILL***, tenderly, as their heads touch.)*

*(***GOTTFRIED*** draws back, looking down at* **BILL** *and* **TOM** *lying entwined on the carpet. Then he slowly rises to his feet.)*

GOTTFRIED. This is not a very good situation.

*(***GOTTFRIED*** steps out through the shattered French doors into the backyard.)*

Martha? Could you come here for a moment? I think possibly there is a problem.

(In the bathroom, **JANET** *turns to* **APRIL** *decisively.)*

JANET. Tell me, April. Truthfully.

APRIL. Anything.

JANET. Have I wasted my life on a mirage?

APRIL. No. You're the only one of us who's tried to do something really big.

JANET. But in the process, is it possible that I may have contributed in some way to Bill getting sick? I mean... *have* I been emotionally neglectful?

APRIL. That's not a productive line of thought.

JANET. Because – well – April, I do have something rather difficult to tell you...

> (**APRIL** *raises her eyebrows questioningly and smiles.*)

APRIL. Ah. I was wondering about that.

> (*In the living room,* **TOM** *gets up, swaying, rushes out through the hallway, and bursts into the bathroom.*)

TOM. Sick. I'm going to be sick.

> (**TOM** *staggers past the two women and vomits into the bath.*)

APRIL. Oh dear!

> (*In the living room,* **MARTHA** *looks down at* **BILL***'s lifeless form then runs toward the bathroom, appearing in the doorway.*)

MARTHA. April, could you come out here for a moment? But perhaps *without* Janet?

> (**JANET** *steps over the prostrate* **TOM***, crashes past* **MARTHA***, who tries to block her way, and runs into the living room, closely pursued by* **APRIL***.*)

> (**BILL** *is lying stiff as a board, motionless as a corpse, on the carpet. And* **GOTTFRIED** *appears to be kissing him, deeply, on the mouth. The kiss of life.*)

APRIL. Interesting development. Either this relationship has evolved with quite extraordinary rapidity or –

> (**JANET** *pushes* **GOTTFRIED** *aside roughly and kneels beside* **BILL***, staring aghast at his lifeless*

*face. Then she starts rhythmically thudding
down on his chest, a woman possessed.)*

JANET. Bill! Bill, Bill...

(One, two, three.)

(One, two, three.)

(One, two, three.)

*(MARTHA and JINNY stand at a distance,
watching, their arms wrapped around each
other as JANET crashes down on BILL's chest
again and again.)*

(APRIL reaches out to hold GOTTFRIED's hand.)

*(BILL coughs at last and comes back to life. He
blinks and stares up at JANET's wild, flushed
face.)*

*(They gaze at each other for a long, quiet
moment like two strangers who are bewildered
by this sudden intimacy.)*

BILL. Janet...how has it come to this?

(BILL reaches up slowly to touch JANET's face.)

APRIL. *(Murmuring softly.)* You know, Gottfried, our
relationship is starting to look remarkably healthy. No
secrets. Just out-and-out disagreement on everything
that matters. Maybe we should reconsider our future.
Will you marry me?

(And then there's the knock at the door.)

(Twice.)

(Everyone freezes.)

(APRIL gasps and turns toward JANET.)

*(JANET sits back on her heels, and her
expression changes from tender concern for
Bill to quiet, controlled rage.)*

JANET. Marianne...

(**JANET** *leaps up. The others try to stop her. But she runs past them with the strength of a rugby player. She runs into the bathroom and pulls the gun out from its hiding place in the laundry basket.* **TOM** *is lying prostrate on the floor by the lavatory. He cowers away from her, shrinking into a fetal position.*)

TOM. Janet, please don't kill me! I'm sorry, I'm so sorry. Please don't kill me. I'm a good person. I'm a good person.

(**JANET** *stares down at him for a moment before rushing out into the hall.*)

(*Then – wild-eyed, trembling – she opens the front door.*)

JANET. You told me you loved *me*! *Me!* You said you couldn't live without me! The two of us, side by side – together – working, loving, saving the health service, saving the country! Oh, Marianne. You traitor!

(**JANET** *slowly lifts the gun, pointing it at the [unseen] arrival.*)

(*Blackout.*)

[MUSIC CUE 12]

End of Play

www.ingramcontent.com/pod-product-compliance
Lightning Source LLC
Chambersburg PA
CBHW070359120726
47909CB00008B/2921